# The Children of the Tribes

By Eva Wasserman Margolis

# Table of Contents

This book would never have been realized without the much-needed help from my husband, James Margolis. His expectations and editing kept me wanting to improve it, and it was quite a challenge to satisfy him.

I thank my editor Susan de la Vergne, and the artist of my cover Heidi Reiter. They are sincere people that care about others.

I thank my illustrator Tharanga Siriwardena from Fiverr.

A big hug and much respect goes to clarinetist, Dr. Elizabeth Crawford for recording and releasing my solo composition, The Children of the Tribes, to her CD: Instant Winners vol.II

Misty Black helped me get through all the issues of bringing the book all together. She answered all my questions and really was a very important part of this process. Formatting by Misty Black Media LLC.

I thank those children of the tribes who came into my soul, asking me to tell their stories. They are my true inspiration.

I thank all those who gave reviews and helped support this book through my Gofundme project. All of you gave me peace of mind, and you believed in me even before most of you read the book!

I am blessed with so much love from across the globe.

I truly owe so much to humanity and the musical world surrounding me.

I am grateful.

# Introduction

If I could help the world, especially our children, how would I do it? What about helping parents? Though I wrote this book for adults, it's really a children's book! This book is a journey into a world that once had powerful rules.

It is a book for all ages and can be read with children at different times in their lives. It's a journey of twelve children. These short stories were my idea to "imprint" or implant good influences before the conflicts of growing up and making choices in society begin.

Like all stories, THIS BOOK IS A JOINT PROJECT BETWEEN THE NARRATOR AND THE CHILD.

So many objects, subjects, medicines, people, programs, and ideas that are marketed these days are detrimental to our children. They take a child in the wrong direction, away from the honorable, compassionate, resilient person they should become.

Yet it is nearly impossible to avoid these influences. Therefore, I offer these stories told by beautiful children, angels who have led me through life. These angels, some of them, were my students. They taught me about myself. When I started to see them being given drugs before they were out of high school and how it damaged them, I knew that this book was needed.

We were all born with natural instincts. Let us try to live as close as possible to who we were born to be. That is what I hope this book brings us: the ability not to lose ourselves, our sense of direction, our ability to act to benefit others. I hope the same for our children that they grow up to have better sense than to follow the nonsense and bad advice that's often put in front of them. That is real freedom. Real freedom is knowing what to do and doing it, making the right choices for ourselves and our world.

Take this ride with your children if you want to make their lives and yours better. It will be a challenge but with lots of work, you and your family will come out winners. My vision of this book came from my experiences.

I have taught and performed on the clarinet for 39 years. During those 39 years, I have seen great players, great human beings, and met others who found their calling in other fields. During the last few years, I have seen a significant decline in critical thinking and passion for something outside oneself. Instead, I see a deepening trend toward self-absorption and a tendency to think continually about me, myself and I. Can a healthy world live on me, myself, and I?

My son and my granddaughters are the gems that I try to keep polishing by influencing them in a way that I think will benefit themselves and their children. My experiences have been my teacher. Judaism has greatly influenced me. The hard-core stuff! I don't judge, I care. I judge myself and became who I am by judging who I wanted to be. I did this by watching others' behaviors.

There are always judgments and answers in every move we make. We depend on the right people to give us direction. This happens until we die.

A Rabbi from Tel Aviv once gave a speech on caring, and there was a progression to his advice. First, you must nourish your body. Then you must nourish your mind. If you don't take care of these, in that order, you cannot devote yourself to your family and the world. What comes after is your family, and they are of secondary importance. Why? If you don't feel well, you can't be devoted to them!

We can then arrive at an understanding of our culture, religion, and the people we identify with. We must take care of the world we live in. We must care about other cultures, plants, and animals. We must care about the little worm that is caught under a heavy leaf.

What I learned from this great Rabbi's story was this: You must follow this progression to create a healthy world. You should not care about the worm before you first take care of yourself and your children.

This book is not about the little worm but the ability to stay sensitive to a world that so needs sensitivity.

Once survival in the world was about finding food, water, and shelter; today's survival is about finding the balance in this world of so many conflicting messages. This "real" world takes work and effort to figure out and navigate! "Synthetic survival" should be the last choice, not the first. I use this term because there are many other means in which to find answers for coping. However, they may be through drugs or through those that may help but may lead you in a direction that is not your own.

Don't be mistaken. Life challenges every human on this earth, even those who seem to be rich and famous. Often fame and wealth are their challenges!

I hope this simple book will make everyone who reads it think about what is most important in life.

If I have offended anyone in any way through these

stories, please forgive me. I will never be able to satisfy everyone everywhere!

If one adult's or child's life is changed for the better because of this book, then this writing was worth all the effort. Children are the future and ours. Education is their future.

May our children find peace on this planet. It is part of your job to help them in this endeavor. The puzzle of life seemingly is getting harder to put together when, in fact,  it is truly simple.

When there is a mom or dad in the story, you can substitute it for whoever is the caregiver. You just need to change the words. Let us have great hope that all children will find their way home. This is my passionate plea to the world.

## Dedication

This book is dedicated to my nephew, Michael Wilner. May he always find the strength to conquer. These stories are also for my young grandchildren, Daniella and Shira. I hope someone, someday will be there to read this book to them as they mature.

# The Tribe of Reuben 1

*Dedicated to: Dina Yaffa and Avital Churi*

My name is Adam, and I was like a prince and treated like one. My ancestors thousands of years ago had many princes, princesses, kings and queens that came from the tribe of Reuben.

When you are the firstborn in a family, there is no one who came before you. Parents sometimes make mistakes with us because they have had no experience raising a first child.

As a firstborn, I was given too much, and even though I was good, I was wild. I thought I should have everything. I thought I knew everything. I had many toys, so many, that my room had no room for me! I also had many pets. My mother cleaned up after them, so she had no time for me. My teeth had holes from all the candy and sugar that I received.

I was a Prince with a lot of freedom, never thinking of helping my mother or father. I needed to be taught how to help. You see, I was never taught to do anything for my parents or anyone. I did things for me. I was a prince and proudly considered only me, myself, and I. But that was something that I was beginning to grow out of as my family was changing.

I did love my family with all my heart and soul and would do anything to protect them. When I got older, my parents had another child, Dina. She was beautiful, happy, and always jumping into the Red Sea. She jumped without fearing how deep the sea was. She jumped without looking at how shallow the waters might be. I took good care of her and watched her with all my soul. With me by her side, she was in good hands!  Growing up made me responsible! Having a sister made me understand responsibility.  You must always take care of your family, no matter what! Dina was lucky. For my parents learned a lesson from their mistakes with me and made sure that she followed more of the rules that help guide a young child.

Family is the core of the entire world. If everyone took care of his or her family, the world would have fewer problems.

Parents must take care of us but also teach us to appreciate all that we have. My parents made my home safe, and I had no worries.  At first, they gave me too much without asking me to give back and show more kindness towards others. Sometimes there is a fine line crossed with children who are given too much, making it appear as if they have too little. Sometimes those who we think have nothing have everything they need. I felt I had everything I needed because I was loved.

**Parents:**

• How can we know what is too much or too little?

• Is too much for one child not enough for another?

• Is there a way to teach a child to be happy with fewer material items and more responsibility for self and family?

**Child:**

• What makes you feel love from your parents?

• Do you think you have too much of something and maybe you would like to give to someone that has less than you?

• Make a list of things that you know you are lucky to have. Then, put the list into a drawer to view it again on another day. Keep Children of the Tribes with you, and maybe one day, you will read it to your own child.

## The Tribe of Yehuda 2

*Dedicated to two Chayas: Chaya Hafkeh and Chaya Raskin*

Hi, my name is David. I am ten years old. I've been learning about my ancestors, people who lived years and years ago. These people, my ancestors, were given so many things to do. These were called commandments. They were commanded to do these things, so they must be very important. In fact, they were given 613 commandments! My parents taught me that I am Jewish and that there are many ways that I need to learn in order to follow all of these commandments. At ten years old, what do I care about? Playing! Of course, my parents let me play, but they also teach me about our people and the meaning of a very important word: "Mitzvah."

What do kids that are not Jewish always tell me? First, they tell me that my life seems hard. They say, "You have to do this, and you have to do that, so many rules!" They also say, "You have to pray a lot. You have to pray before you eat. You have to pray before you sleep, and you have to follow Sabbath."

To them, our Sabbath seems so difficult to understand. Our Sabbath starts Friday night and goes until Saturday, just as it becomes dark and you can see three bright stars. Sabbath is an evening and a day, where Jews don't do anything considered work. We don't even turn on our phones or computers. We don't turn on the lights. We even have a special refrigerator that shuts off its inside light for 24 hours!

Following Sabbath is not difficult for me because I have done it all my life. My parents say Sabbath is beautiful. Many people say this.

Why is Sabbath so beautiful? Because my family spends almost every minute of the day together! It seems to some that this is strange. My friends tell me they think it's strange, but they also say they like the idea and tell me that they appreciate me and see that I have a special quiet about me. I am glad.

My friends' parents like me too. I think they appreciate me because I don't want to hurt others or make them mad. It's just how I am. I also like to share, and I think they like that too.  They really love it when I share my mother's home cooking! It's more fun to give than to take. I've learned this. It makes me happy.

Mitzvahs are required from the one who created all that we see and hear.  As Jews, we believe in creation. We believe in rules. My parents can't explain why these laws matter because, to someone my age, they just say you must discover this for yourself. Time will prove their beauty.

My mother and father say, "Commandments are gifts and are the greatest treasures that exist. They are even more important than playing!" Wow! What could be better than playing? However, my parents say, "This great treasure takes time to receive, and it takes hard work. This treasure can't be seen or touched." I am still young and think, "Doesn't everything take patience and hard work?"

My parents tell me that this treasure you will receive is not something you can ever actually touch, much less navigate. What does it mean to navigate? It is like a maze, and you try to find your way through this maze because if you get to the end, a gift is waiting for you! This maze starts when you are born and you go through it for years and one day it becomes clear where you are. You get to the end of the maze. Some of us get to the end of this maze sooner than others. Some never  get to the end. Yet, we're all trying to navigate this maze and make the world a better place. This is what my parents tell me. They say that if we all followed the commandments to better living, the world would glow.

What's important, my parents say, is that we all must try to be the best that we can be. We must be an example for the world. We must show that besides playing all of the time (which I love to do), we also need to think about ourselves as if we come from a storybook, a story about the right way to live. By following the right way to live, we control how the story goes!

What is good? What is bad? What is right? What is wrong? The answers are not always blowing in the wind! The choices we make need to be learned and then practiced over and over again. Some of us need them like water, yet some of us have already discovered them!

I want to be around children that respect me for being "good." Unfortunately, some parents teach my friends that it is best to be the winner all the time. They teach that if you don't look out for yourself, then someone will take what should have been yours..

If every child was like that, just wanting to win, just looking out for themselves all the time, they'd be no fun to play with. I don't think I'd like myself very much either if I was like that. Would you?

My Mom and Dad say to me, "We are older and wiser than you." Children need someone to help them as they grow older. We need someone to tell us that we are free to choose what we want to do. We need to know we have the right to choose which direction we will go. We can choose to help others if we desire. In fact, it's so important that we make the right choices because the right choices help this world. The children of my generation have a lot of responsibility to make good decisions.

We need to know how to choose. We need to know what free choice is so that we, the children of this generation, make good decisions! Good decisions come from parents who have good judgment. This is where education and knowledge are so important. The maze is here! This is what we must navigate!

**Parents:**

• How can you explain to your children the difference between right and wrong?

• What happens when parents don't directly teach their children the difference between right and wrong? If your parents did not teach you what is right or wrong, how can you find the answers?

• Does the word "rules" or "laws" bother you? Imagine a world without them. Not all of us need rules and laws, but some of us would destroy the world without them.

**Children:**

• What treasures do you have?

• How do your parents help you to make good decisions?

• Is it possible to care about someone else as much as you care about yourself? Is there anyone you feel that way about?

## The Tribe of Issachar 3

*Dedicated to my sister Monica Wilner and her daughter Erica.*

My name is Netanel, and I'm 8 years old. Since I was about five, I have been very curious about all living things. I ask my mother and father many questions, and sometimes I ask other relatives as well.. Some questions they can answer and some they cannot.

I am going to ask you some questions that so far

nobody could help me with. Maybe you can, or maybe your parents.

See if you can help me:

When we see a house, we know that someone built it. Do you agree with that? So when we look at this beautiful world, why is it so difficult to figure out who built it? The world has so many parts to it. It was much harder to create than a house, that's for sure.

The sea is gigantic, yet it does not swallow up the land. Instead it throws waves on to the land as if to remind us that it's here. Sometimes when I sit on the beach I think how fun it would be to drive with my parents to the bottom of the ocean. Have you ever thought about doing that? Can we?

When I lay on my back in a field and squint at a cloudy sky, I look at the many shapes of the clouds overhead. Why do they all look so different? Are they all different? Are there any two that are ever the same?

During the day we have the sun to warm us and at night when the moon is up, sometimes its light guides us when we walk around outside. Is the moon at night like a big lamp for everyone in the world? Why does light, especially at night, make us feel safer before we go to sleep? Is my nightlight really just a small moon that has come into my room to comfort me?

How can small birds, with such small bones in their feet, survive cold, heat,  wind, and also sit  on the electrical wires without ever worrying about that at all?

But here's my biggest question, which nobody has answered: Why do some people who have so much, still seem so unhappy?

I am grateful for the little things around me and the people I have in my life. I ask my parents sometimes how I can make the world a better place.  Is there a recipe, or formula that I need to follow? What do I need to learn? Will the light from the sun and moon always guide me?

**Parent:**

• Is it important to teach your children that science is not absolute and that over the years, many theories change?

• If your child is thankful, does it mean that you are doing a good job?

## Child:

• What are three things you like to learn? Write them on a piece of paper and post them over your head and think about them before you go to sleep.

• Are you thankful to have people around that love you? If so, go and hug someone you love, and don't tell them why!

• What are some of the things you love?  Can you hold all of them in your hand, or are some of them held tightly in your heart?

• What is in the world that you think was made by man?

## The Tribe of Zebulun 4

*Dedicated to my friend Mira Bornstein*

My name is Gaddiel. I come from the Tribe of Zebulun. My best friend is Netanel, from the Tribe of Issachar. He is my best friend because he is wise and smart. I think he is wise because he always tries to understand the WHY of things? Why do we need food? Why do we need sleep? Why is there good and bad in the world? His "WHYS" never stop!

25

Both of our tribes lived near the seacoast and worked together, as we do now.  We are connected to the sea. The seacoast changes greatly with the sun, sand, and  storms. At the sea, you can see all the way to forever and breathe fresh air from distant places. The tribe of Zebulun and I are people who travel on small boats to catch fish that feed the Tribe of Issachar and my friend Netanel. We know that studies are really important, so we try to help them have more time to study. Sometimes we even prepare their food for them! Then they are free to spend more time with books, and their education helps our lives. Their learning makes our lives more exciting and more advanced for all twelve tribes.

Netanel is a born leader and knows the answers to questions that most adults do not have answers for. Or they don't have time to answer. Netanel studies most of the day, but than later on he has time and we can play. I'm always happy when that happens.

My parents like Netanel and are very happy that he is my best friend! He teaches us to be pleasant. He says that, even though we are young, we have to look for the right way to live. WHY? Because later on bad habits and behaviors are hard to change, so don't start now! If children choose the wrong path, it makes problems in the future for ourselves, our parents, and even our society. I love Netanel and so do all that meet him, BECAUSE, he cares about those that he loves and he shares the light of his learning with others. Sharing is loving. Sharing is caring. Sharing brings wisdom to others.

Someday, we will be adults. We will have responsibilities. Netanel teaches us how to play, how to make friends, how to listen to others, and how to help others. He shows us how to know what is right and not right. He teaches us what is healthy and what is clean.

Life is sometimes confusing, but I like to think it is one giant learning experience. My parents tell me that they are still learning every day. And they are adults! They tell me we never stop learning, even if you live to be 100.

In the past, the Tribe of Issachar traveled from one tribe to the next to illuminate the world. Light is made up of all the colors of the rainbow. It brightens our world with goodness and hope. His tribe of Issachar, helped to illuminate the world with study.

Good is what we all search to find deep down. However, we should never accept the excuse that there is a reason to hurt another child, human being, animal, or plant unless it's to protect ourselves from harm! If we do argue or fight, it should never be with fists, but just with words, and the words should come from wanting to help the other person. Sometimes tough words are needed if we care.

In the eyes of the twelve Tribes, everyone is equal when they are born.

**Parents:**

• Reflect on what is both right and wrong in our world today.

• What is the difference between being fair and being moral?

• How does respect for others look?

**Child:**

• Do you pick friends because they make you happy or sad?

- How do you show respect towards others?

- What does "wise" mean to you?

## The Tribe of Naftali 5

*Dedicated to Meirav and Shomron Koush*

Attention: "Mother" can be replaced with any caregiver to the child.

My name is Debra, and my ancestors came from the tribe of Naftali. When I was three, I imagined so many stories. I dreamed about how mothers all over the world would come together. They all wanted their children to be happy. I saw the future, and it was fresh and bright.  Mothers made sure our neighborhoods had flowers and trees, and that our homes and streets were clean. The mothers all grew vegetables because they thought it was essential to eat right! These mothers helped each other, and each child helped their mother.

I saw all of this from my little bed, and I saw it happening all over the earth. Mothers made sure that every child was taken care of for one reason alone: they were their mothers, and they worked together in harmony, just like music!   One mother would work, and another would take care of her children. That was their first concern, always the children. Everything else took second place. These mothers believed there would be enough food for everyone as long as it was shared by those who had more.

The mothers taught me that if one person does not have enough food, it is the same as those who have too much. They can both make you sick but in different ways. That's why people who have too much should give to people who don't have as much.

The children of Naftali's tribe, my ancestors who were my family long ago, grew up secure and strong way before I was born. But their mothers had a different lesson to teach their children! Studies, in those days, were different. You studied to survive. You studied to support your family. Sharing and trading were more important than money. Their homework was learning to hunt, fish, build homes, grow crops, cook, and make bread, skills necessary in order to live!

I am now ten years old and still dreaming dreams, but why are they just dreams? The truth is, mothers today don't have the time to share their lives as they do in my dreams. My ideas and dreams are strange to others. My friends say they dream about watching a new TV show or playing games on their phones, iPads, and computers. I am very confused. Why are my dreams so different?

Our birth mothers on our street that are not in my dreams tell us they have to work so hard because they want to give us many things! They also want many things themselves. I say to my mother, "My dream is not to have things. I just want to be with you, Mom! I need you to be with me right now. I want to be with you when I'm sad. I want to be with you when I'm happy. I want to go to you when I'm hungry so that you can prepare something healthy. I want to share my childhood with you."

I also said, "Mom, I don't like coming home every week with a cold, a skin rash, an eyesore, or a bruise. How would you like to feel uncomfortable almost every day? You ask me many times why I don't act so nicely? Maybe because I am not feeling well. Listen to my dreams, Mom. They speak to me from my elders thousands of years ago. They are the dreams of both truth and love."

You can't always achieve your dreams, but you can reach for other dreams. Never stop dreaming.

**Parent:**

• What were your dreams as a child, and how are they similar or dissimilar to your children's?

• What key factors help you understand your child's behaviors, and what may you sometimes misread?

• How do you teach your child to share with others?

• Why are those who have too much to eat as dangerous as those who don't have enough food?

**Child:**

• How do you let your mother know when you are unhappy or feeling sick?

• Would you prefer to read a book with your mom or dad or watch TV?

• What does the word "harmony" mean?

## The Tribe of Gad 6

*Dedicated to my dear father of blessed memory, Eric Joseph Wasserman, and his first cousin, Lou Bravmann, who was a light in my life after my father passed away.*

My name is Eliasaph, and I have a story for you about my love for my grandfather and grandmother, who helped take care of me when I was young.

My grandfather did many things for me. I'm told he changed my diapers. He gave me my first pacifier and called it "PT." He made me happy. When I got older, he

35

was so important in my life. He cared so much about me that I could feel it in every one of the 206 bones in my body.

My grandfather and grandmother came from Russia to the Land of Israel. They both came from the tribe of Gad, a tribe that existed a long time before they were born. That's a long time ago! Think about how long the tribe of Gad was around before I was born!  These tribes first lived in the land of Egypt and waited for hundreds of years before they could enter the Land of Promise.

Both of my grandparents had dreamed of leaving Russia to go to the Land of Israel. How did they find themselves in Russia in the first place, if their families from long ago had already been in the land? One day when you are older, you may want to discover this true story of the twelve tribes that were spread across the world. This story can be found in every language in the world and has been around for more than 3000 years!

My grandmother's dream to return was powerfully strong, which was true for my Grandfather as well. They had strong roots that one has in their ancient lands. It was as if they heard distant calls in the silence of night calling them home. Have you ever dreamed about an ancient land that you felt was where you wanted to travel? It's an inner voice. It is a warm feeling deep in your heart.

My grandparents only had one son. When he was a young man, he went to fight in a war, and he never came back. He was my father, and I was born only after he died. He was brave. He died because he was saving many soldiers who were hurt in the fight. My grandfather was always very sad about this, but my grandmother somehow found a way to make peace in her heart. She helped raise me, shared her happiness with me, and sometimes spoke about being sad.

She missed my father too. She always said that I was the young tree with the best roots. She would tell me that life is about beauty and about being safe. You have to have strong roots when life is not always full of roses. She says that when she is around me, she is happy. My mother was like one of those red roses in a garden! She was beautiful but when I would be too stubborn, she would prick me and she would turn bright red just like a rose! My mother loved me even when I would be hard to handle and she loved that I could be  sensitive. To be sensitive is a gift, always work on it and never be afraid of it.

I love my grandfather very much. He is good to me, and I hug him all the time, but he never seems to be content. Why do I love him then? Because he is showing me how lucky I am to be happy. His unhappiness made me work hard not to be like him! He is teaching me to always look for the positive even when I am sad.

Sometimes we can learn from our family. We learn to try to be like them when we admire what they're doing. We also learn not to be like them when we don't admire their actions. We still love them even if they have some problems. We have them too!

My grandmother taught me to be happy but in a different way. She taught me to pray. She taught me there are many prayers, and if you say them every day, you will never feel lonely. Even if  you are alone, you will never feel alone! She said prayers when there was lightning in the sky and then we saw a rainbow. She taught me to look at  clouds to see all kinds of shapes and sometimes colors! She even saw the good in scary things and said prayers  that would protect others even if  she was not present! They were not  scary movies but natural events like hurricanes, tornadoes and earthquakes. She cared about others so much. Because she cared about others, she was loved by so many!

She also said blessings for being alive. She taught me to be thankful for the ocean filled with lots of fish for us to eat. She prayed because she was grateful to God for creating me!

She said prayers to protect the family and everyone all over the world. She was even thankful for the gift of each person being designed differently from her! She said blessings for our dog. She said blessings for the trees. She said prayers because she was glad to have the knowledge to be able to say prayers! She was thankful when people recovered from being sick, and she said prayers then. She said prayers for the world so that it would become a better place.

She told me that when you're grateful, you are happy

because you appreciate what you have been given! Blessings and prayers every day make us aware of everything that should not be taken for granted.

All these blessings were a part of her life, and today they are part of mine.

I am just a child, and though I am happy most of the time, I think if you love someone, you should not make them unhappy. Just love them. It will make you happier!

**Parent:**

• What were the twelve tribes? Can you find the answer?

• Can blessings and prayer done sincerely bring your children happiness?

• How do children of today's world learn the difference between right and wrong?

• How do we know the difference between right and wrong?

• What if one child thinks something is right and another child thinks it is wrong?

• What if every person in the world made up his own rules?

• Why should death be acknowledged when telling a story to young children?

• How can believing in God help your child to grow?

**Child:**

• What is a "tribe," and do you belong to one?

• What is the difference between war and peace?

• If someone has great sadness and then tries to make you sad, what can you do?

## The Tribe of Asher 7

*Dedicated to Nima Pulturak*

I am lucky.

My name is Ayelet, and I'm a young girl from the Tribe of Asher. The tribe I come from goes back thousands of years. It was not a large one. But the girls in this tribe were considered the most beautiful. Their beauty was in their hearts. Like everyone, their hearts beat in their chests, but unlike most people, their hearts beat to the rhythm of music. It was full of joy and belonging. They were joyful about life, grateful to be alive. Some of us think that gold and silver are the most expensive and beautiful things we can have. But gifts from the heart, a heart filled with gold, are way more valuable. I also love music and I play the clarinet. Music is my life and my heart beats with beats of love to express not only the beats but the feelings I have when I play. I would rather have music in my heart any day then all the gold in the world.

Thousands of years ago, King David was the second of many of the tribe's kings. He also had many talents that came from the heart, such as poetry, hymns, dance, music, and psalms. And he was full of love for all the children of the tribes! He played with soul, and so do I! He played harp.

King David wrote many psalms. Psalms are sacred songs and hymns. Sacred describes something seen with great respect by a religion, group, or person. A hymn is a song, text, or other composition that praises or celebrates a human being, event, or something else that's important. King David and the psalms he wrote remind us to feel thankful for what we have and not to be jealous of what we don't

I play the clarinet, and when I do, I feel his presence and the presence of many others from thousands of years ago. Back then, they had no speaker systems or videos to record their playing. I am sorry dear children, King David cannot share. However he has left his psalms and wisdom that has gone from mouth to mouth for many generations.

King David was a caring King, and he believed in God with all his heart and soul. Still, he was human. He tried to be perfect, but of course this was impossible.

I want to teach you what King David taught me . The history of people and their past can help us to grow because we can learn from their mistakes, and we can be inspired by their successes. We can take from our history and make it colorful. We can always choose experiences from our history and make them better. Our past can tell us a lot about our future, but our future is never past.

My tribe's experiences have taught me lessons. They were all written down years ago. They were first spoken, one person to the next, by those who wanted the best for their society. Perfection is not about the present, but with HOPE, WORK, EDUCATION, and LOVE, we may find it in our future.

Maturity is when we search for the best we can be, even with all of life's challenges. We learn through our experiences.  Being different and unique comes from working hard. We can achieve this by pursuing many different types of work, work that makes us proud. Work that makes us love ourselves and is good for our surroundings and the world.

Work is fun if we love it!

If the world is a stage, what character do you want to be? What kind of work do you want to do in this world? What kind of contribution will you make? You could be an artist. There's music–so many types of music, so many musical instruments. There are all kinds of art, paints, and palettes. You could build, design and create, designing houses, jewelry, write software, build furniture, and so much more. You can lead travel expeditions, scuba dive to the bottom of the seas, or hike up to the Tibetan Plateau. You can make others laugh, feed the poor, assist people in making healthier food and medical choices. You can become a great surgeon. You can grow plants and raise and help animals.

Even if those things seem a long way from where you are now, there are other things you can do right now. You can thank the postman and the man that takes the trash off your street. You can visit your neighbor who lives alone.

Fight for a cause you believe in, but with love and not hate. If you believe in God and you want to share this with others, it should be done with kindness. It takes a deep commitment if what you believe in is important. If you love your neighborhood, make sure it stays safe. Make a promise that you will always find people to help you keep it safe.

I am a young girl, but I already know what I want. I want to make our community better. Every society that takes on a good cause makes the world a better place. It is a sign that the community cares. It is a sign the future will be better.

Some people think they can be different by bringing

attention to themselves by acting crazy, or even doing damage to others or even themselves. But they find they are never satisfied by the outcome. Satisfaction is feeling good. It adds up over time. Fighting and arguing with others is harmful, even worse when the fight is not worth the battle.

Now is the time to grow. Look for the good in the world, and follow the rainbow of colors that bring happiness to your childhood. Your parents can take your hand and help to lead you to unforgettable experiences. They love you more than anyone on the planet.

**PARENT:**

• Explain something you see as beautiful to your child and help them to understand why you feel this is so beautiful.

• Tell your child something that you are passionate about, and then tell them about something you feel deep compassion for, to help them understand how compassion and passion are similar and different.

• Think about a "crisis" your child had over the last few weeks. Discuss this with your child and come up with a list of how they might address this in the future. Post this list and the solutions you both came up with in their room.

**Child:**

• Tell your parents about something that you love and try to explain to them why you love it.

• What is one thing that you care about that is not living?   Can you explain to your parents why you love this thing so much?

• What is one thing you have done in your life that you felt was so important?   Discuss this with your parents. Was it for a "cause"?

## The Tribe of Levy  8

*Dedicated to Joni Davidi and my mother who passed away in 2009 Kitty Wasserman.*

My name is Miriam. I am from a tribe that, thousands of years ago, wandered from Egypt to a land of milk and honey. That's what it's called because the land is a good place to provide you with everything you need. Our tribe was dedicated to honesty and faithfulness. I have been called the child who has "the eyes of a bear and the heart of a deer." I have come to you to sing, and all I want to do is sing! But coming to your time period, so many years after my own, has made it, for some reason, impossible to sing! I can only reach you, children of the future, to bring you a message. What is the news? Can you guess? What is so essential that I have to travel to your time to tell you?

There are lots of messages I have come to share!

I once built a house of clay. My friends and I loved to play in it! We loved to be outside in a place like our clay house to rest and pretend. That's where I learned to sing. I used to sing to the trees. I was such a happy child. I was never embarrassed about being joyful. I learned that, even if you don't have a clay house, you can build a house in a tree or make a special place on the ground under some bushes with blankets. (Ask your mom or dad to help you make a place like this.) You can also use a tent. In my world in the past, tents were not made in beautiful colors as they are today. Now you can have beautiful tents, in blue and green, even orange. Go out and have some fun!

We the Children of the Tribes all have messages for you, and we care about you children of our future in different ways. I'm here for only one reason: to find ways that you can learn and use, to make you happy, now and always.

Do you know what the past is? The past can even be just yesterday! I come from many years before you were even in your mother's stomach! We had games and hobbies that were very different from yours.

For you, children of today, you love computers and anything where you can push buttons. Many of you don't have a place to go outdoors to play. I used to love to play outside. I loved to play ball, to run, and even discover new waterfalls. I loved to walk up mountains and fish with my father and mother. Sometimes my mother was too busy, and so I went only with my father. I loved the fresh air. I'd see birds and sometimes deer and bears! I heard water flowing through streams. It sounded like words being spoken, or even sung! I also heard wind whistling through the trees. These sounds made my heart so glad. I loved beaches and lakes. I loved nature.

Today, you can find nature on your computer. You can see these places, but it's not the same. What you see is real, but you can only see it! Sometimes it is even called "live" but... it's not the same as feeling the wind on your skin, or feeling snow falling and even tasting it, or watching a fish jumping from the sea and hearing it splash back into the water. The smell of the sea makes you want to swim for miles and miles. It's not the same as actually going to a garden of roses and sneezing because the smell is so powerful! These are all adventures essential to our senses. What is "sense"? It's to feel and to feel life!

Children, these adventures are so good for your soul! Food, clothing, and a place to sleep are not enough.

How do you find beautiful adventures like these? You need someone to take you there.

Thousands of years ago when I lived, I once had to walk for 40 years in the desert, and it was beautiful, but I missed the smell of green grass, the singing of birds,, and the sound of flowing water. Enjoy children. Enjoy! Tell everyone that nature is what you want to feel! Tell your friends! Tell your family! Tell them that children need time in nature to help our imaginations grow, to hear its sweet sounds, to taste a fresh berry or a banana, or even milk a cow. This will bring music to your hearts. Be joyful!

**Parent:**

• How can nature improve our children's moods?

• If children don't get enough movement and exercise, what happens to their spirits?

**Child:**

• How do you feel after a day hiking or playing at the park?

• How does the sun feel on your face?

• Why do we need to protect nature?

• What is the most beautiful thing you have ever seen?

• Does Miriam truly care about you when she shares her message? How do you know?

## The Tribe Of Joseph 9

*Dedicated to Dalia Reshef*

My name is Gilead. My mom is a woman of honor and peace. My father is a man of wisdom. Thousands of years ago, their families lived in a culture of amazing people, and they all loved each other, even though on some days  it seemed impossible.  Don't all our families have impossible days sometimes? Do you always get along with your brother or sister? Don't partners or moms and dads also have arguments? Do you always get along with your friends?

Today I am eight years old, and I have traveled back in time, thousands of years ago, to be with my family from the past. My mother wished me back in time. Why? Let's see.

I am the only one of all the tribes who travels back into history.

Living thousands of years ago seems in many ways the same as today. Just like now, people are always in a hurry. I had told my mother many times that people push ahead of me when I go to stores. They are constantly rushing to get someplace. They dash around so quickly that they don't even have time to think of what they are supposed to be doing. They are so rushed that they make me rush too.

Thousands of years ago, where I am now, well, it's the same feeling!

However, in this time, thousands of years ago, rushing around is about looking for food, hunting, and riding on horses. It's also to get wood for fires and oil for burning lamps. People are rushing around to survive, getting the things they need in order to live.

It's also about getting ready for winter or summer. It's about finding a place to store food so it will not spoil. There are no refrigerators here, thousands of years ago.

People and families argue here in the past as well. Their arguments are about having enough food, preventing diseases, and making sure they have the proper clothing for hot and cold weather. These arguments come from worries.

Traveling into the past, and now sharing these experiences with you, makes me appreciate your lives and mine even more. Here, thousands of years ago, there are no hospitals, no air conditioners, no heaters. There aren't many musical instruments either. But they do sing! There are no movies to see, and so these children from the past watch others act on a stage. They don't feel they are missing anything! Many of the paints, crayons, and markers that we could paint with today did not exist. Do you understand how lucky we are today to have so many colors? They were happy and we should be too. We have so much more and our lives are so much easier.

Thousands of years ago, when people argue, there is no place to hide. They have only one room. For some people it is just a cave!  So they learn to get over it and live with each other. There's no choice.

Wow! I just returned to my present world. Our world. The world where I have a comfortable bed, air conditioning, heating, and lots of toys, not to mention a TV. However, with all this, everyone is still rushing. My parents have two cars, which go a lot faster than the way people got around thousands of years ago. And yet, they are still always rushing. Thousands of years ago, there were no cars, just donkeys, horses, and camels. That's the world of my ancestors! I am glad I am back with my mom and dad. I appreciate what I have.

I am sensitive to all these feelings and experiences. My father also tells me that I am sensitive. He says it's a gift. It helps me to understand other people.  He says sensitivity is a sign of being smart in many ways. However he says that sensitivity is  not only about what you feel but what others feel too!

My father can see the person behind the face they

present to everyone around them. Sometimes these people, who are sometimes even family, are rough to others. I was sensitive to this as well and did not respond well to them. However, my father had tolerance and compassion for them and taught me as I grew up to be more thoughtful.

He says, "Such people seem hard on the outside because their lives may not be easy like yours and mine. It is not an excuse, but it also means that we live with a group of people that allow others to be different and sometimes not so nice to each other. It means we love others with both good and bad characteristics. We are like a big family that still has lots of growing to do." My father teaches me that sometimes these rough people could also be the kindest. You can see this he says and I see it is true, during a time of crisis.

What is a crisis? It is a day that is unusual. It could be a day we are sick or needy. It could be many different events, but most crisis activities are when we need support as an adult or a child. What is valuable to learn is that it's about someone being there for you, your family, or the people in your society. They care about you when life is not going so well.

Just think how many good days we have compared to the bad ones. We are all so lucky, and how would we know what a good day was if we did not have some bad ones? Did you ever think about that?

What I learn from my mom is to never judge a book before you've actually read it. Don't just go by the first couple of pages. Get into it. There are so many different people in our world. There are so many cultures. Only those who live with each other know each other. You can't figure out other people from far away. Only those who are family members truly know who their children are and who they may become.

I also learned from my mom that education at home is essential. My mother continues to teach me, first, to judge someone only after you get to know them. Don't judge somebody the first minute you meet them. Have patience, and you may discover that they could be your best friend one day. This seems to be just like getting into a new book!

Second, she says, help everyone in the world who

does not hurt or steal from others. There is no excuse for stealing and harming others. If everyone stole and injured others, there would be chaos in every home. There would be chaos everywhere. What is chaos? It is what it sounds like! Chaos!

Sometimes, you may be taking a chance, meeting somebody new, and getting to know them, but it's better to take a chance than live in a world where no one takes chances. What would the world be like?

We are so important to each other.

The real angels in our world are those who are there when you most need them. They come along when you don't expect them to be there. If nobody helps each other on this globe, then we'll all be in big trouble.

Don't be afraid to be kind.

**Parent:**

• What do you teach your child?

• Everyone in life is given at least one challenge? What are yours?

• What would humanity be like if nobody cared about other people?

• Teach your children the word "chaos." Give them examples of its meaning.

**Child:**

• What is a woman of honor? What is a man of integrity?

• What is it like to do good things for others? How do you feel?

• Do you have good friends? What is a good friend?

• What does it mean to care?

## The Tribe of Simeon 10

*Dedicated to the wanderer James Margolis, my husband*

My name is Aviatar. I am from the tribe of Simeon, and I have a powerful desire to travel. Today we have planes, trains, and cars! But thousands of years ago people moved from place to place on foot or by horse and wagon. It took them so much longer! I don't care how long it takes me to get where I want to go. I will make it.

There are so many places that I dream of going. My parents say that if I eat healthy foods, then I will be strong enough to go all over the world. So every day I eat fresh vegetables, grains, and delicious berries! My parents tell me that with lots of good food in my body, I will grow to be able to climb high mountains and swim in the deepest seas.

I know that by traveling the world, I will learn about different people and the ways they live. I will meet people I can help, because I really want to help the people I meet on my trips. If something terrible happens in another country, I want to be one of the first to arrive so that I can help the people there. I want to build houses for the poor and teach students who live far from schools.

Thousands of years ago, there weren't schools, as there are today. My parents tell me there are many children in the world who do not have enough to eat. No school and not enough to eat.  It makes me sad. I want to help children who are hungry.

I'm going to bring my adventures back home in pictures I have taken of all the places I have traveled.

Do you have a camera? Cameras are fun, and today you can take them everywhere. Once there were no cameras, and after a trip we had only what we could write down or remember. Pictures are so easy now. I want my country to grow, and I want the people of my country to learn from others so that we can continue to be a good example.  We must always continue to learn. In the past, our tribes were sent to Babylonia from Israel as slaves. Today Babylonia is Iraq. It is a country in the Middle East. In the time of the Bible, before we were sent to Babylonia, all our tribes were also slaves that lived in Egypt.

Maybe that's why I want to travel. I'm not sure where I came from. I do know one thing: My tribes are the people of the book. We are scattered all over the world. One day, we will all be together as a family. We will do our best for ourselves and society by working hard to create a better world for all people. All people have that responsibility– to take care of others, and not to cheat or harm them. In fact, human beings have a duty to take care of each other. No one can take away that responsibility from us.

Maybe one day we will all be responsible for each other, working together in harmony like great music. It's my dream of a better world. Don't ever be afraid to fight for a better world.

**Parent:**

• Does your child appreciate small things in life?

• Has your child been on a camping or nature trip?

• Has your child ever planted a seed and watched it grow to maturity?

• Have you ever taken a short course on nutrition? What about your children's doctor?

• Have you taught your child to be responsible for his home, surroundings, and the world?

**Child:**

• What do you eat when you are hungry?

• Where is the Middle East? Can you find it on a map?

• Have you ever worked with an old-fashioned globe and located where you are on this planet?

• What is "responsibility"?

• Why do people travel?  What do you think they are looking for, and what do you think they want to take back to their homes?

• Some things can be bought, and some cannot. What things that cannot be bought do people take home with them from trips?

## The Tribe Of Dan 11

*Dedicated to children of the globe. They are our future.*

My name is Samson, and I am a powerful child. That's what people tell me. I have a mother and father who pester me all morning, day, and night because they want me to eat well.

They both prepare healthy meals for me and do not bring sweet drinks home for me or even candy. Yet worst of all, I cannot leave the house without brushing my teeth. They refuse to let me out the door!

I am strong, and I was named after Samson, who lived thousands of years ago. Do you know what made him strong? His hair! Once his hair was cut off, he lost all his power.

Back then, there were no toothbrushes, but there were no sweet drinks either or candy that would fill in the spaces between your teeth.

Parents used to make almost every meal for their children! They made healthy meals from healthy foods because that was all they had! They had no refined food or preservatives, whipped cream, or ice cream! (I still wonder how they cleaned their teeth, don't you?)

In today's world, my parents have it hard! Why? They have to fight with everyone, so that I will have food to help me grow physically and mentally. Food that is not nutritious can even give us children diseases as we get older. But my parents are not really fighting with everyone, they are fighting for me. It sometimes seems to them like they're fighting a losing battle because when I watch TV, I see sugary foods, and then I want them. If I walk down to the store with my parents, there are racks upon racks of sweets. Even when we go to the gas station, all we see are sweets! Do you know what kale chips are? How about dried apples? Do you like blueberries in your cookies instead of chocolate chips? Blueberries are sweet too, but they also give you vitamins that help your body grow. Chocolate chips... not so much.

When I was really young I learned that my parents were right when arguing with me. I have to admit to you the truth! Here is what happened: I went to a friend's home and dove into their candy, like I was diving into a delicious swimming pool on a hot day. Then we went to the movies, and I ate junk food from the first minute until the final credits left the screen. I ate and ate and then came home and felt sick and weak. My stomach hurt all night! Did this ever happen to you? The next day I got a cold.

My parents were different. They cared enough to fight for my good health and tried  to give me good sense. They knew that when I danced the crazy dance that I had gone overboard and guzzled down too much soda and munched on too many candy bars.  I sometimes ate until my belly was as tight as a drum.  I ate until my tongue could no longer feel my teeth but only the coating of the candy I had last eaten.

Now I am more than strong, I am smart.  I have learned to eat nutritious foods. I have become like a scientist doing the greatest experiment. When I ate only the healthy foods my parents made, I found I was not only stronger but that I could learn better.

If I had never eaten good nutritious food, well, I would not have known the difference! As I  began to understand this, I believed my parent's words, and thanks to them, now I can jump and run faster. I am also one of the smartest kids in class. I noticed that many of the smart kids also were doing some kind of exercise so I decided to exercise too.  The most amazing thing happened: I could focus better on what I was learning! I was stronger than I ever expected to be!

 I hope as you get older, you will be able to control what you eat or be able to tell through your body which foods make you feel good. You know that great sports people eat a lot of nutritious foods to make them strong. That's because the body needs good food. Food that has protein, fiber, and vitamins. Some examples are  nuts, vegetables, and fruits.

It wasn't just eating junk food and feeling terrible that convinced me to eat better! It was a dream I had. One day I fell into a deep sleep, deep as the Dead Sea. I was on the highest mountain after a great flood, and in this sleep, I saw myself where no child had ever been. There in my dream, I saw what I would look and feel like if I continued to eat the wrong foods. It was a nightmare.

Looking good is not important these days because being overweight has become sort of normal. But being overweight can bring many diseases later on in life. It's a scientific fact.   But think about it: who cares later in life what happens to you and your body? Your parents care. Now I do too. You should care more than anybody because it's your body!

My parents tell me that hard love is sometimes the best, the kind of love that tells you the truth even if it's hard to hear. "Discipline," is not a popular word these days, just like belief in God has lost popularity.

Sometimes love is about not giving up! My parents always loved me enough not to give up.

While up in the clouds on this very high mountain, I realized by looking down upon the world, how right my parents were! Some parents think it's better not to nag and pester their children so they can just seem to be friends. Are parents supposed to be your friends? More importantly, should we always do what most people are doing? Is it always in our best interest?

I was named Samson, and I want to stay energetic, helpful, and make the right decisions as I grow older. My parents love me more than they love themselves. I know that for sure. Who loves you the most in the world? Your friends or your parents? Sometimes it is best to listen to the one who does not always tell you what you want to hear! I am proud to be guided by my parents. I am strong!

**Parent:**

• Share with your children the people you have admired most in your life and tell them why.

• In what ways can discipline be an act of love?

• What does a parent risk most when they don't take

the time to make sure their children are eating healthy foods?

• What is your vision for your children? Do you love them enough to stop those around them from changing your children's destiny? This can sometimes be the greatest fight for your child's life.

**Child:**

• Can you tell us what foods make you feel good, and what kinds make you feel bad?

• Do the parents of your friends cook food you like? What kind?

• Do you have dreams? Tell your parents about them.

• What does it mean to exaggerate?

• What does it mean to nag?

• What is admiration?

## The Tribe of Benjamin 12

*Dedicated to Daniel Bar Tov*

My name is Abidan, and I travel this world with my beautiful dog Meshi. His fur is as soft as a Persian carpet made from the most beautiful silk. His black coat is darker than the desert at night in Egypt. It is even darker than the sea at night when the moon is nowhere to be found. Yet, when the moon comes out of hiding, it shines on Meshi's coat like a million jewels.

Meshi makes me laugh, and she helps me to love. She is devoted to me and gives me security when she sleeps next to me each and every night. She is my friend and protects me when  darkness comes and locks out the light. Sometimes at night, I hug Meshi tightly, and our dreams circle us.  I am only eight years old, but one day I will take my compass and set out with Meshi to chase our dreams. I am so lucky to have her friendship and love. She brings smiles to all she meets. She is important to me. She is family. She teaches. She loves without anger. She is faithful.

I am young, but I am filled with passion.  I dream one day of helping animals who are hurt or even lost.  But my mother says it is more important to help people than to help animals. I have a dream, and my friends also have ambitions. My friend Sharon wants to be a nurse, but her mother wants her to be a famous violinist. My friend Daniel wants to be a chef, but his father wants him to be a lawyer. I tell my mom that we are young, and we have come into this world for a purpose. All of us need to have our dreams.

If we want something positive, then why should our dreams be taken away from us? We are all only eight years old! In the end, as long as we are doing something that does not harm the world, why can't we dream? We don't want your dreams; we want ours . Thoughts create passion, and with love, we know our direction in life!

**Parent:**

• Why is this tribe's message the last one in the book?

• What is passion?

• How do we become the best parents we can?

• If we had a childhood that was not easy, how can we improve our child's lives without having our own experiences affect us?

• Can we use our experiences, good and bad, to make us better parents?

• If we know that we have bad influences in our lives that affect our parenting, should we find every possible way to break away from them for the sake of our children?

• Share with your child your greatest childhood dream

• If you are brave, tell your child why it did or did not come true.

**Child:**

• What are Persian carpets?

• Where is Persia, and what is it called today?

• Where is Egypt?

• What does "purpose" mean to you?

• What do you love to do?

• Do you love to do that because your friends enjoy it too?

• Do you love it because you see it on TV?

• What do you dream of becoming one day?

• Which kind of animal do you love the most? Do you have a pet?

• What can you do at your age that can help others?

# Summary:

**Dear Children:**

*Dedicated to Vasso Stamatopoulos and Heidi Reiter
They live so far yet they are, and will always be, so close.*

To you, children of today: I am hoping that your generation will help the next generation to grow and prosper. This book is about making your lives better by remembering what truly makes us happy. Happiness is about experiences, about exercise, about family, about love, and about being secure. Happiness is about clean air, fresh food, freshwater, rain, sun, warmth, and even a bit of cold. Happiness is a good computer game or TV show that helps us grow. To be happy is helping and accepting help. If you can give, you have the world in your heart.

It is simple: what we have, no matter how much, it should bring us a smile. Real happiness is a gift but it is never a constant. It's also called satisfaction or being grateful. Some of us are born happy, and for some of us, it is our biggest challenge.

What if there were no happy people around us? How would we know what happiness is? Work– all of you!- on making the world a peaceful world. Happiness starts with you. You can't help others find happiness if you never find it yourself.

These Children of the Tribes are here to help you find your way. You can read these stories during all periods of your life. I hope the children you meet in these stories will continue with you in your heart, and continue on from one generation to the next. May these stories be a part of making you more beautiful as you all grow into adults who love life, for love is the answer.

To the adults reading these stories: may you always remember and preserve the child within you.

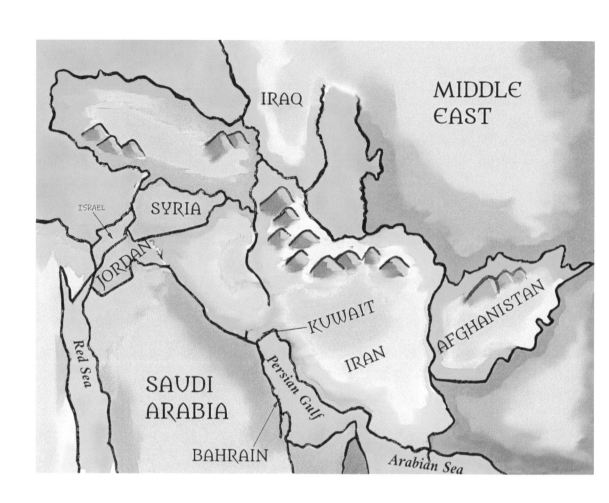

Lightning Source UK Ltd.
Milton Keynes UK
UKHW050822090223
416624UK00003B/343